P9-BIA-447

Ebb & Flo

and the
Greedy Gulls

Jane Simmons

ALADDIN PAPERBACKS

New York London Toronto Sydney Singapore

To Celia

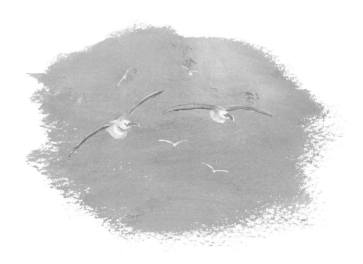

First Aladdin Paperbacks edition May 2003

Copyright © 1999 by Jane Simmons

ALADDIN PAPERBACKS
An imprint of Simon & Schuster
Children's Publishing Division
1230 Avenue of the Americas
New York, NY 10020

All rights reserved, including the right of
reproduction in whole or in part in any form.

Also available in a Margaret K. McElderry Books for Young Readers hardcover edition.

First published in Great Britain by Orchard Children's Books
First United States edition, 2000
Manufactured in Singapore
2 4 6 8 10 9 7 5 3 1

Library of Congress Catalog Card Number 99-62216
ISBN 0-689-82484-X (hc.)

ISBN 0-689-85810-8 (Aladdin pbk.)

It was a lovely day.
Ebb listened to the seagulls laughing.
Everything was wonderful.

Ebb closed her eyes and sniffed the sea air.
Beep, beep, said Bird.
The seagulls laughed.

Ebb snoozed on the warm sand.

The seagulls woke her.
Woof! Woof! barked Ebb.
The seagulls just laughed.

"Ebb!" said Flo. "You've eaten
all the sandwiches!"
Beep, beep, said Bird.
The seagulls laughed.

"You've eaten loads," said Flo. "Oh, Ebb!"
"Oh, Ebb!" said Mom.
Beep, beep, said Bird.
The seagulls laughed and Ebb sulked.

Ebb sulked in her favorite spot.
It was so unfair.

It began to rain. Mom and Flo
cleared the food away.
The seagulls swooped.
Waves lapped at the boat.
Ebb sulked.

"It's the seagulls! *They're* taking the food!" cried Flo.
"Shoo!" shouted Mom.
Beep, beep, said Bird.
The seagulls laughed.
Ebb sulked.

When Ebb looked up, she was all alone.
The little boat was drifting out to sea.
Woof! Woof! said Ebb. But nobody came.

The little boat started to spin.
Woof! Woof! said Ebb.
It went around
and around, faster and . . .

. . . faster and FASTER.
Woof! Woof! Woof!
barked Ebb.

CRASH!

"Where are you, Ebb?" shouted Flo.

Ebb looked up and there were Bird and Flo.
Beep, beep.
"Oh, Ebb," said Flo, "I'm sorry I blamed you."

"I do love you so much," she said.
And the seagulls laughed overhead.